MW01248836

CLASSIC CARS

AN IMAGINATION LIBRARY SERIES

THE STORY OF

Ferrari

by Jim Mezzanotte

GARETH**STEVENS**
GS PUBLISHING
A WRC Media Company

Please visit our web site at: www.garethstevens.com
For a free color catalog describing Gareth Stevens Publishing's
list of high-quality books and multimedia programs,
call 1-800-542-2595 (USA) or 1-800-387-3178 (Canada).
Gareth Stevens Publishing's fax: (414) 332-3567.

Library of Congress Cataloging-in-Publication Data

Mezzanotte, Jim.
    The story of Ferrari / by Jim Mezzanotte.
       p. cm. — (Classic cars: an imagination library series)
    Includes bibliographical references and index.
    ISBN 0-8368-4533-1 (lib. bdg.)
    1. Ferrari automobile—History—Juvenile literature. I. Title. II. Series.
TL215.F47M48   2005
629.222'2—dc22   2004059112

First published in 2005 by
Gareth Stevens Publishing
A WRC Media Company
330 West Olive Street, Suite 100
Milwaukee, WI 53212 USA

Text: Jim Mezzanotte
Cover design and page layout: Scott M. Krall
Series editors: JoAnn Early Macken and Mark J. Sachner
Picture Researcher: Diane Laska-Swanke

Photo credits: Cover, pp. 5, 7, 9, 11, 13, 17, 19, 21 © Ron Kimball; p. 15 © National Motor Museum

Printed in the United States of America

1 2 3 4 5 6 7 8 9 09 08 07 06 05

Front cover: **No matter what year or model, Ferraris are usually fast and exciting—and bright red.**

TABLE OF CONTENTS

Words that appear in the glossary are printed in **boldface** type the first time they occur in the text.

THE PRANCING HORSE

Enzo Ferrari loved car racing. He lived in Italy. In the 1930s, he led a team of race car drivers. They raced cars made by Alfa Romeo. Every car had the team **emblem**. It was a black **prancing** horse. It came from a famous fighter pilot. The team won many races.

After World War II, Enzo started his own car company. It was called Ferrari. The new company made racing cars. The cars began winning races. Ferrari made cars for regular driving, too. The prancing horse appeared on these cars, just like the race cars. They were very fast. The prancing horse soon became famous!

Ferraris have changed a lot through the years, but the prancing horse still appears on every model. This Ferrari F50 was built in 1995.

FAST CARS

In the 1950s, Ferrari racing cars won many races. The cars were bright red. They had powerful V-12 engines. The engines had twelve **cylinders**. The engines were in the shape of a "V."

Ferrari kept making street cars. A few were **exported** to the United States. The cars were expensive. They were mostly built by hand.

These cars were not very **practical**. They were almost like race cars. They were hard to drive in traffic. They cost a lot to fix. But they were also fast and beautiful. It was exciting to drive a Ferrari. Many people wanted to own one!

This Ferrari Barchetta was built in 1949. Like many Ferraris, it has a V-12 engine. Barchetta means "little boat" in Italian.

POWER AND BEAUTY

What is the most beautiful Ferrari? Some people think it is the 250 GTO. Ferrari began making this car in 1962. The car could be used on race tracks or regular roads. A person could race the car and then drive it around town!

The GTO is a light car with a powerful engine. The body is made of thin **aluminum**. Leaning on the car might dent it. The body is like a **sculpture**. Ferrari only made about forty 250 GTOs. Today, a 250 GTO can sell for millions of dollars!

In the 1960s, the GTO won many sports car races. This GTO was built in 1962. You can drive it on regular roads, but it was made mostly for racing.

THE DAYTONA

In 1968, a new Ferrari came out. People called it the "Daytona" after a racetrack in Daytona, Florida. In 1967, Ferrari race cars won a race at Daytona. The cars came in first, second, and third!

This car had a big V-12 engine. It was very powerful. The Daytona was the fastest street car in the world!

The engine in the Daytona was in front. Ferrari race cars had engines behind the driver. They were **mid-engine** cars. After the Daytona, things began to change. Ferrari began making mid-engine sports cars.

A powerful V-12 engine sits beneath the Daytona's long hood. By the mid-1970s, the fastest Ferrari sports car had its engine in the middle.

A FERRARI CALLED DINO

What Ferrari is not called a Ferrari? The Dino! Ferrari began selling the Dino in 1969. It was named after Enzo Ferrari's son, Dino Ferrari. Dino died when he was just a young man.

The Dino did not have the Ferrari name. It was less expensive than other Ferraris. The Dino was a mid-engine car. The engine was right behind the seats. The V-6 engine was smaller than other Ferrari engines.

But the Dino was still a Ferrari! It was fast and fun to drive. It was beautiful, too!

The Dino was smaller and less powerful than some other Ferrari models. But it was still very fast. The engine sat sideways behind the seats.

THE POPULAR FERRARI

In the 1980s, a Ferrari starred on TV. This car was the Ferrari 308 GTS. It was used in the TV show *Magnum P.I.* Magnum is a **detective** in Hawaii. He gets around quickly in his Ferrari!

Ferrari started making this car in the 1970s. It replaced the Dino. It was a mid-engine car, too. It had a new V-8 engine. This Ferrari was less expensive than other models. Many more people could afford to buy it. The 308 was very popular.

The 308 GTS has a top that can be removed. In the 1980s, many people watched this model on Magnum P.I. Many people wanted to drive one, too.

THE REDHEAD

A new Ferrari came out in the 1980s. It was called the Testarossa. At the time, it was the fastest Ferrari. *Testarossa* means "redhead" in Italian. Parts of the engine were painted red.

The Testarossa was a mid-engine car. The engine was a flat-12. It was not in a "V" shape. Instead, it was flat and square. It sat low, so the car handled better.

Most cars have one **radiator** in front. The Testarossa had two radiators in back. There was one on each side. The Testarossa looked different from other cars!

The Testarossa has an unusual look. The ridges on its side take air to the radiators in back. In the 1980s, a Testarossa could be seen on the television show Miami Vice.

FIFTY YEARS OF FERRARI

Enzo Ferrari died in 1988. His company kept making fast, exciting cars. In the 1990s, the company built the F50. This model was built for the company's fiftieth anniversary. The company only made 349 cars of this model.

The F50 is a street car. But it is almost a race car! The engine came from a racing car. It has a lot of **horsepower**. The F50 is not good for everyday driving. The engine is right behind the driver. It is very loud. There is no radio. This Ferrari was built for one thing — driving fast!

The F50 has a wing in the back. This wing helps keep the car on the ground when it is going very fast.

A CAR FOR ENZO

The Enzo is Ferrari's newest **supercar**. It came out in 2002. It is named after Enzo Ferrari. With a name like Enzo, you know this is a special Ferrari! The car is built with carbon fiber. Carbon fiber is used in the space shuttle. It is light but very strong.

The Enzo is a mid-engine car. You can see its big V-12 engine through the rear window. Some people say the Enzo looks like a **Formula One** car. It can go more than 200 miles (320 kilometers) per hour. Enzo Ferrari would be proud of this car!

Like earlier Ferraris, the Enzo has a big V-12 engine. The car has many special features, including doors that swing upward.

MORE TO READ AND VIEW

Books (Nonfiction)   *Ferrari. Enthusiast Color* (series). Dennis Adler (Motorbooks International)
Ferrari. Hot Cars (series). Lee Stacy (Rourke Publishing)
Ferrari. Ultimate Cars (series). A. T. McKenna (Abdo & Daughters Publishing)
The Ultimate Classic Car Book. Quentin Willson (DK Publishing)

Videos (Nonfiction)   *50 Years of Ferrari.* (Kultur Video)
Automotive Series: Ferrari. (Brentwood Home Video)
Ferrari. (A & E Home Entertainment)
The Ferrari Collection: Ferrari Dino 246 (Kultur Video)

PLACES TO WRITE AND VISIT

Here are three places to contact for more information:

Ferrari Club of America
P.O. Box 720597
Atlanta, GA 30358
USA
1-800-328-0444
www.ferrariclubofamerica.org

Galleria Ferrari
Via Dino Ferrari, 43
41053 Maranello
Italy
39 0536 943204
www.galleria.ferrari.com

Petersen Automotive Museum
6060 Wilshire Blvd.
Los Angeles, CA 90036
USA
1-323-930-2277
www.petersen.org

WEB SITES

Web sites change frequently, but we believe the following web sites are going to last. You can also use good search engines, such as **Yahooligans!** [www.yahooligans.com] or **Google** [www.google.com], to find more information about Ferraris. Here are some keywords to help you: *308 GTB, 365 GTB/4, barchetta, Dino, Enzo, F50, Ferrari, Formula One, GTO, Maranello, and Testarossa.*

auto.howstuffworks.com/enzo.htm

At this site, you can learn more about the Ferrari Enzo. The site has many pictures of the model, including views of the engine and the interior.

www.allsportauto.com/english/ferrari.php

Visit this web site for a variety of photos of many different Ferrari models.

www.carsfromitaly.com/ferrari/index.html

This web site has a history of the Ferrari company, plus information and pictures for Ferrari models, from the earliest cars to the latest ones. It also has links to other sites.

www.empirestateregion.com/cars.htm

Visit this web site to learn about the history of the Ferrari company and to see pictures of a variety of Ferraris, including current race cars.

www.ferrariclubofamerica.org

At this web site hosted by the Ferrari Club of America, you can see photos of many Ferraris.

www.ferrariusa.com/Welcome.html

This web site has information and many photos for all of the latest Ferrari models.

www.ferrariworld.com/FWorld/fw/index.jsp

At this official Ferrari web site, you can learn about both Ferrari street cars and Ferrari racing cars.

www.qv500.com/ferraritrp1.htm

Visit this site for information about the Ferrari Testarossa and three nice pictures of the car.

GLOSSARY

You can find these words on the pages listed. Reading a word in a sentence helps you understand it even better.

aluminum (uh-LUME-in-um) — a lightweight metal 8

cylinders (SIL-in-durz) — tubes inside an engine where gas explodes, giving the engine power. 6

detective (dee-TEKT-div) — a person who solves crimes or finds out information for other people. 14

emblem (EM-blum) — a picture or design on something that lets people know it belongs to a certain group or company. 4

exported (EX-por-ted) — sent to other countries to be sold. 6

Formula One (FORM-you-luh WON) — the rules for building a certain kind of racing car, which goes around tracks with a lot of turns. 20

horsepower (HORS-pow-ur) — the amount of power an engine makes, based on how much work one horse can do. 18

mid-engine (MYD-en-jin) — having the engine in the middle of the car, behind the seats. 10, 12, 14, 16, 20

practical (PRACK-tuh-cull) — good for everyday use. 6

prancing (PRANS-eeng) — jumping up from the back legs, like a horse. 4

radiator (RAY-dee-AY-tur) — the part of a car that helps cool the engine. 16

sculpture (SKULP-chur) — a piece of art that is not flat like a painting and is often made of wood, stone, or metal. 8

supercar (SUE-per-kar) — a sports car that is very powerful and fast. 20

INDEX